Richard Scarry's
Cars and Trucks and Things That Go

HarperCollins *Children's Books*

car-plane

THE 3 MOVERS

TENDER, LOVING AND CARE

moving van

CLEANSING DEPARTMENT

dustcart

dustbins

Richard Scarry's
Cars and Trucks
and Things That Go

fuel oil tanker

FUEL

Have a nice trip!

breakdown truck

MISTRESS MOUSE REPAIRS

garage

mail van

Ma and Pa and Pickles and Penny Pig are going on a picnic. Here comes Ma with the picnic basket. Please hurry up, Ma.

MAIL

mailbox

SADIE'S ICE CREAM PARLOUR

TOYS

SODY-POP

soft-drink truck

The Pigs are going to the beach to have their picnic. But first, Pa has some shopping to do. He is going to order some things to be delivered to their home. I wonder what those things could be?

station wagon

vintage sportscar

shoe delivery car

SAM'S SHOE SHOP

meter maid

pharmacy delivery car

ABC GLASS COMPANY

TAXI STAND

opping trolley

taxi

bookstore delivery van

glass-window truck

veteran car

motorbikes

STOP

Did you see that? Dingo Dog has knocked down almost all the parking meters. What a terrible driver! I think Officer Flossy is going to give him a ticket. At least, she is going to try. We'll see if she succeeds.

baby pram

officer flossy and her bicycle

a frightened parking meter

a terrible driver

sailing dinghy

hay wagon

delivery truck

statue

MICHAEL ANGELO SCULPTOR

HAY

STOP

SOAPY SUDS WINDOW CLEANER

window cleaner

pickle truck

veteran sportscar

Dingo drives off before Officer
Flossy can give him a ticket. Oh, that
Dingo is so naughty! Go get him,
Officer Flossy.

MILK

milk van

dragster

Pa Pig drives past a truck carrying
a statue. "Did you see who is in the back
with the statue?" Penny asks Pickles.
"Yes," says Pickles. "It's Goldbug.
He shows up almost everywhere."

alligator car

steam locomotive

guard's van

flatbed trailer

MOLASSES

tanker

tilt-cab truck

Where is Goldbug now?
Is he riding in the locomotive?
Is he riding in the veteran car?
Can you find him?

tractor

go-cart

veteran car

three-wheel beet truck

canvas-cab truck

dumpcart

unicycle

sports coupé

MISTRESS MOUSE REPAIRS

The Pig family drives by a broken-down truck.
"It won't be broken down for long," says Pa. "I saw Mistress
Mouse working on it. She can mend almost everything."

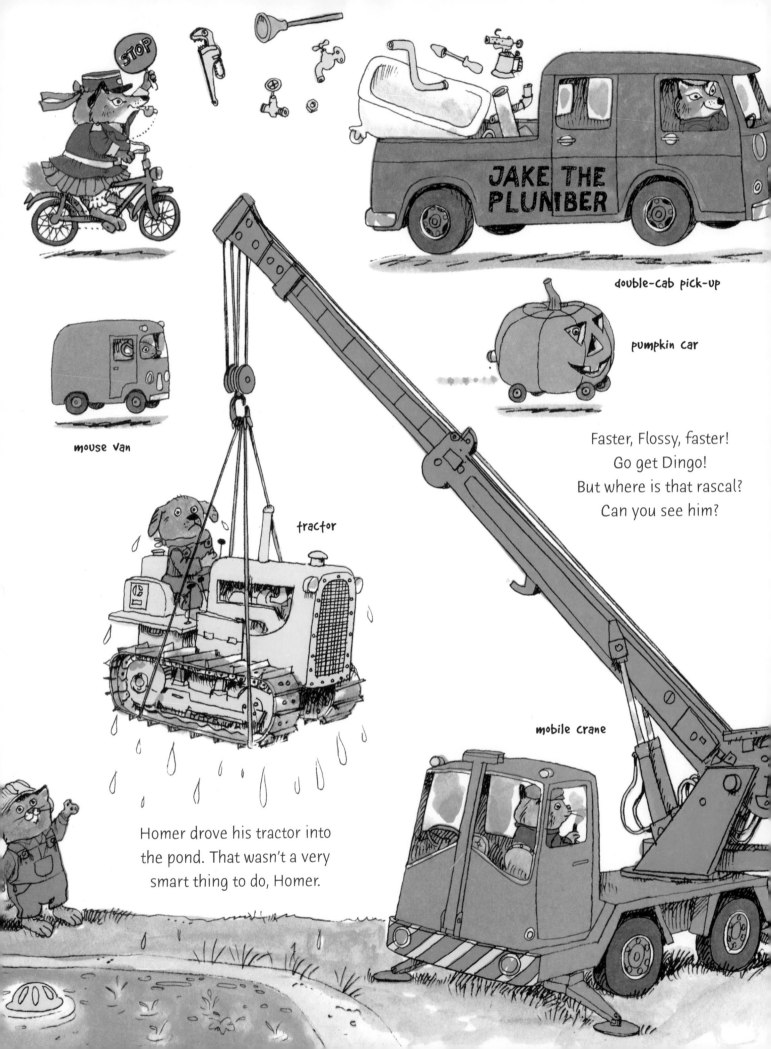

JAKE THE PLUMBER

double-cab pick-up

pumpkin car

mouse van

tractor

Faster, Flossy, faster!
Go get Dingo!
But where is that rascal?
Can you see him?

mobile crane

Homer drove his tractor into the pond. That wasn't a very smart thing to do, Homer.

bus

wooden station wagon

Look! There is Mistress Mouse again. And this
time she is towing a BREAKDOWN TRUCK!
Hello there, Goldbug… wherever you are!

pig van

MISTRESS MOUSE
REPAIRS

a wrecked car being towed by a BIG BREAKDOWN TRUCK which is
being towed by a little breakdown truck

awning

YOUR FRIENDLY CAR DEALER

IRONMONGER

SALE of NAILS

new car

pavement

cement mixer

MISTRESS MOUSE REPAIRS

Now what?
Charlie the carpenter has just bought a bag of nails.
There was a hole in the bag.
Now there are holes in almost all the tyres!

hammer car

SED CARS

used car

school bus

hard hat

SCHOOL BUS

flat tyre

veteran open car

STOP

Where's Dingo? How did he manage not to get a flat tyre? I see Officer Flossy is riding on the pavement. Keep after him, Flossy! Hello, Goldbug…wherever you are.

elevated tower truck

trolley bus

bug bus

SIGHTSEEING TOURS

sightseeing bus

motor scooter

yellow   violet

brown

orange

red

blue

green

pink

PAUL THE PAINTER

a painter's pick-up truck

drain cleaner

ditch-digger

mobile crane

SQUEEZE LEFT
ROAD CONSTRUCTION
AHEAD

ant bus

hot-dog car

rumble-seat sportscar

coupé with open back hatch

Pa is worn out from changing the tyre.
He is taking a nap in the back seat while Ma drives.
All right, everyone! Slow down! There is road
construction ahead.

coupé with open sun-roof

gravel truck

asphalt oil spreader

stone spreader

buggy

Look out! Rollo Rabbit's steamroller has run away. Crunch!
Crunch! CRUNCH! It has squashed three cars flat.

Look out, Flossy!
Look out, Mousie!
Look out, Ma!
Don't get squashed, too

a runaway steamroller

guard rail

roller

road stripers

The workers are finishing the new road.
The last thing they have to do is paint the dividing lines.

KEEP LEFT

FRESH EGGS

motor caravan

egg truck

AIRPORT LIMOUSINE

airport limousine

motorcycle

motor scooter

tandem

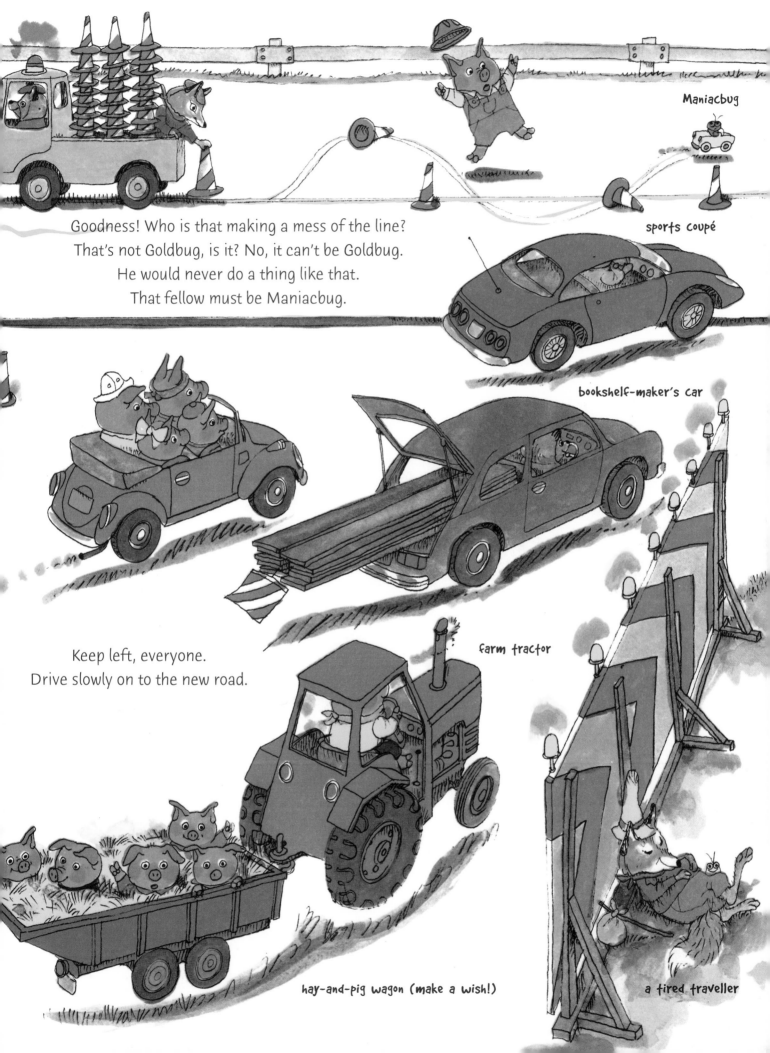

Goodness! Who is that making a mess of the line?
That's not Goldbug, is it? No, it can't be Goldbug.
He would never do a thing like that.
That fellow must be Maniacbug.

Keep left, everyone.
Drive slowly on to the new road.

Maniacbug

sports coupé

bookshelf-maker's car

farm tractor

hay-and-pig wagon (make a wish!)

a tired traveller

veteran car

mini-bus

STOP

IN →

toothbrush car

petrol tanker

PETROL

petrol pump

hose

car washer

REST ROOMS

a woodchuck in a hurry

CAR WASH

mini-jeep

canopied vintage car

toothpaste car

EXIT

oil cans

attendant

Ma Pig sees that they are running low on petrol,
so she drives into the petrol station to fill up the tank.
I can find Goldbug, but I can't see the Pig Family.
Where do you suppose they have gone?

dirty station wagon

lift

car greaser

hook-and-ladder truck

rescue truck

ALL RIGHT!
Who left the
water running in that
fire engine?

water tower truck

fire alarm box

siren

fire Master's car

hose

The Pig family is refreshed. The petrol tank is full again, and Pa is back at the wheel.

nozzle

ambulance

Ladybug has a fire in her car and the firemen have come to put it out. Can you guess who called them?

helmet

bell

pumping truck

fire point

diesel locomotive

mail wagon

tanker wagon

goods wagon

forklift

All the wheels need to
oiled so they won't sque
Squeaky Mouse says so

veteran car

Tom Turtle's car

gardener's truck

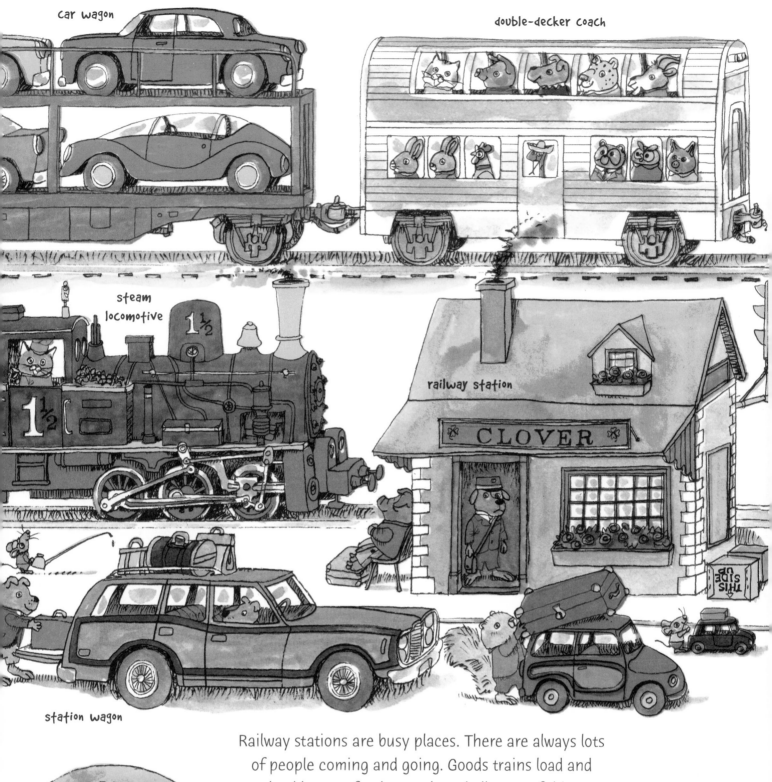

car wagon

double-decker coach

steam locomotive

$1\frac{1}{2}$

railway station

CLOVER

THIS SIDE UP

station wagon

DOUGHNUTS

doughnut car

STOP

Railway stations are busy places. There are always lots of people coming and going. Goods trains load and unload letters, food, parcels and all sorts of things.

"I am hungry," says Pickles. "I am too," says Pa. "Now just be patient," says Ma. "It won't be long before we have our picnic. But first we must stop at Grandma Pig's farm and buy some fresh corn."

corn picker

hay gatherer

At Grandma Pig's farm, all the farmhands are very busy.
They are picking corn, gathering hay and delivering milk.
They are harvesting wheat which will be made into bread.
Grandpa is cutting the grass and Grandma is clanking aroun
on her old steam tractor. My! What a busy farm!

milk cans

corn car

Auntie Pastry and Cousin Willie are selling fresh corn.
It looks so good, Pa just has to take a bite.
"No, Pa," says Ma. "Don't eat it yet! Wait until I cook it!"

FRESH CORN

well

grain harvester

wheat

tractor

Grandma's steam tractor

grass cutter

Wolfwagon

swimming tank

swimming jeep

landing craft

desert jeep

motorcycle and sidecar

tractor motorcycle

General Nuisance's car

half-track troop carrier

water jeep

jeep

Won't you please wake up, Mister Soldier?

tent

bridge

The Pigs have bought their co
and are on their way to the bea
for their picnic. They are passing
army camp. Look at all the soldiers

chapel truck

canteen truck

radio truck

old-style tank

ambulance

old armoured car

tank

army car

gun tractor

civilian car

Look at all the soldiers!
These soldiers are going home for the weekend
to visit their families. Their car is just like an army car,
but it is painted differently.

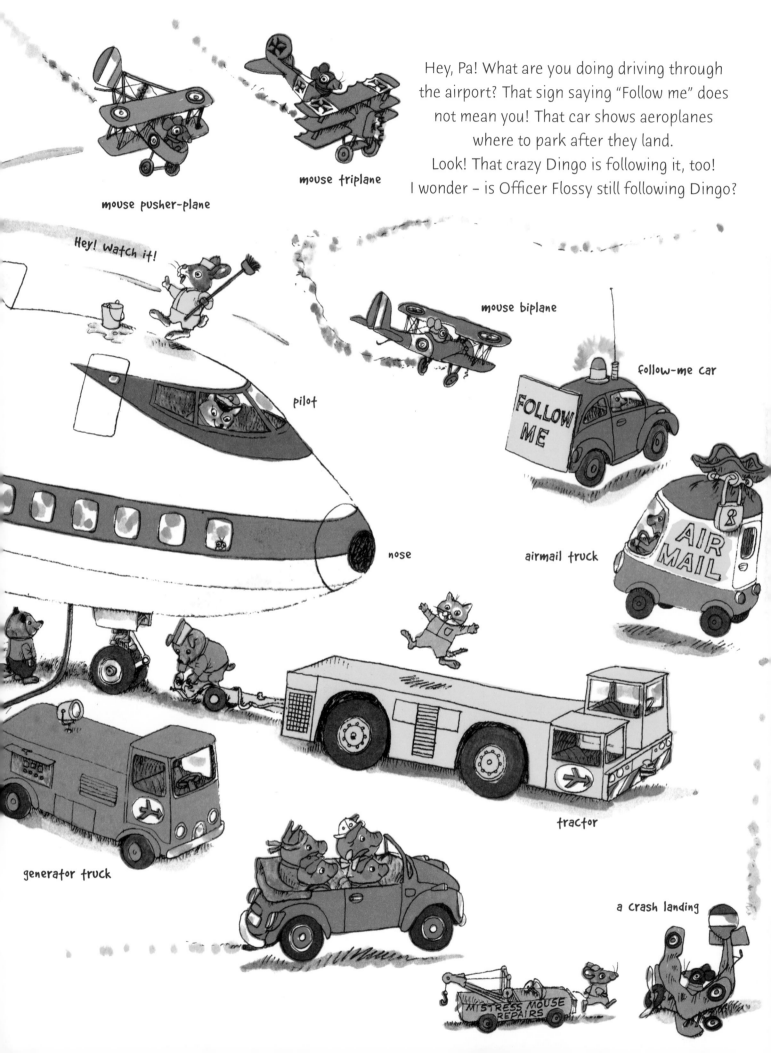

mouse pusher-plane

mouse triplane

Hey, Pa! What are you doing driving through the airport? That sign saying "Follow me" does not mean you! That car shows aeroplanes where to park after they land.
Look! That crazy Dingo is following it, too!
I wonder – is Officer Flossy still following Dingo?

Hey! watch it!

mouse biplane

follow-me car

FOLLOW ME

pilot

nose

airmail truck

AIR MAIL

tractor

generator truck

a crash landing

MISTRESS MOUSE REPAIRS

shark car

ice-cream

ICE CREAM

sand dune

mouse beach buggy

Oh, Piggy, you made a mistake!
Your car won't run in the water. Only a
propeller car can do that.

sand yacht

propeller car

fringe car

BATH HOUSE

shower

refreshment stand

beach buggies

roll bars protect the driver in case the buggy rolls over

"AT LAST!" says Ma. "We are at the beach and we are going to have a nice quiet picnic. Pa, maybe you should put a shirt on. I think you are getting sunburned."
"Oh, I'll be all right," says Pa.

go-anywhere buggy

pedal boat

submarine

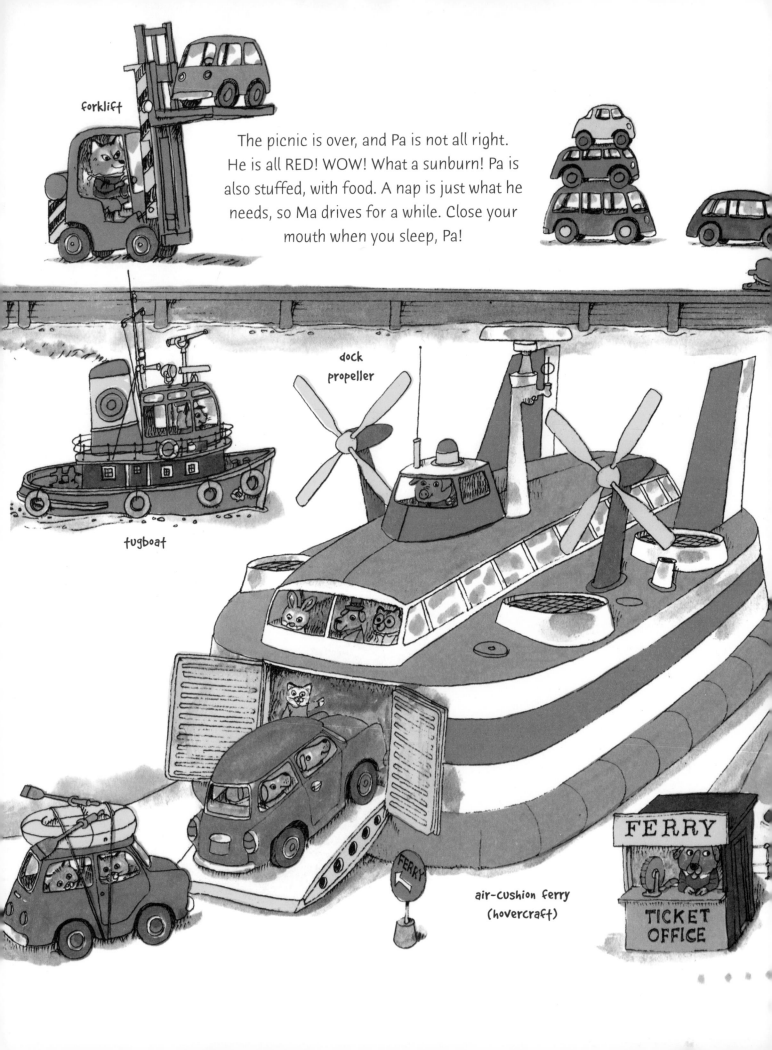

forklift

The picnic is over, and Pa is not all right. He is all RED! WOW! What a sunburn! Pa is also stuffed, with food. A nap is just what he needs, so Ma drives for a while. Close your mouth when you sleep, Pa!

dock
propeller

tugboat

air-cushion ferry
(hovercraft)

FERRY

TICKET
OFFICE

FERRY

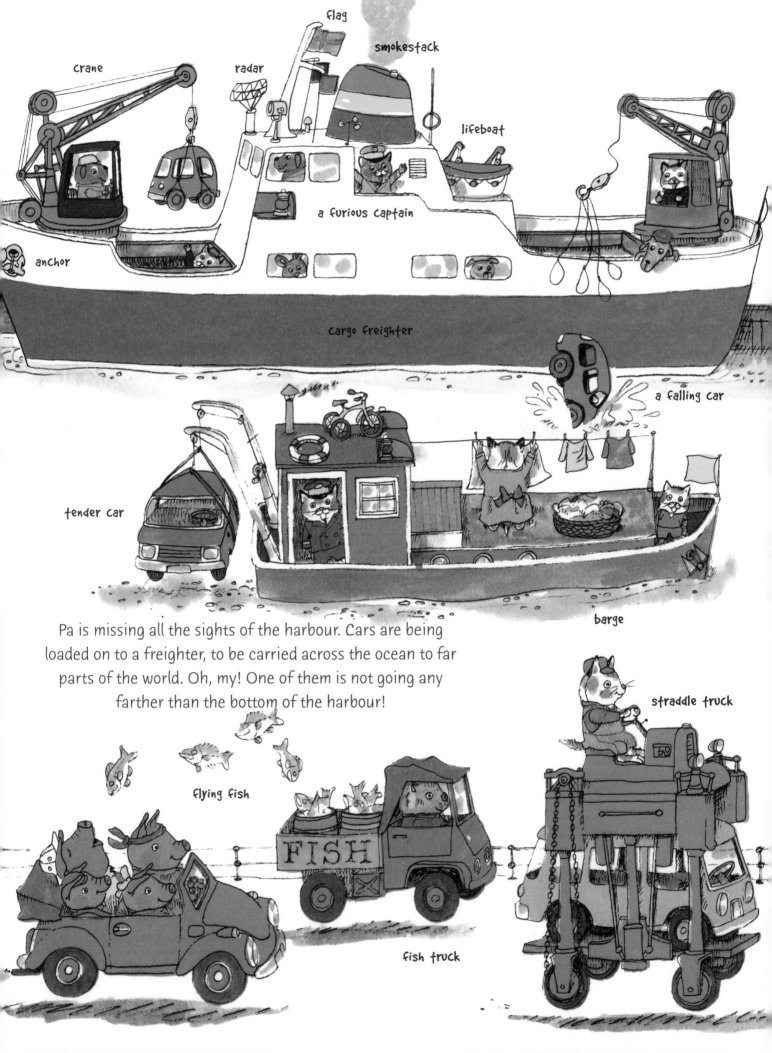

crane

flag

radar

smokestack

lifeboat

a furious captain

anchor

cargo freighter

a falling car

tender car

barge

Pa is missing all the sights of the harbour. Cars are being loaded on to a freighter, to be carried across the ocean to far parts of the world. Oh, my! One of them is not going any farther than the bottom of the harbour!

straddle truck

flying fish

FISH

fish truck

The Pig Family is driving up into the mountains.
It is getting colder. It is snowing. The road is icy.
The pie truck skids off the road.

icy road

a skidding pie truck

bent sign

SLIPPERY WHEN WET

MOM'S PIES

Mistress Mouse says it is time to put on snow chains.
Hey, Pa! Wake up! Put on your snow chains! And please
put the top up.

MISTRESS MOUSE REPAIRS

a worker stringing wire
on telephone poles

TELEPHONE COMPANY

spool of wire

telephone truck

snow bus

Ma put on the snow chains. Ma put the top up.
WOW! Just look at all that snow! Isn't it beautiful?
There's a pile of things all covered with snow in the
truck behind the Pigs. I wonder what they could be?

Harry dear! You must remember to close the window after you!

snowplough

sledge

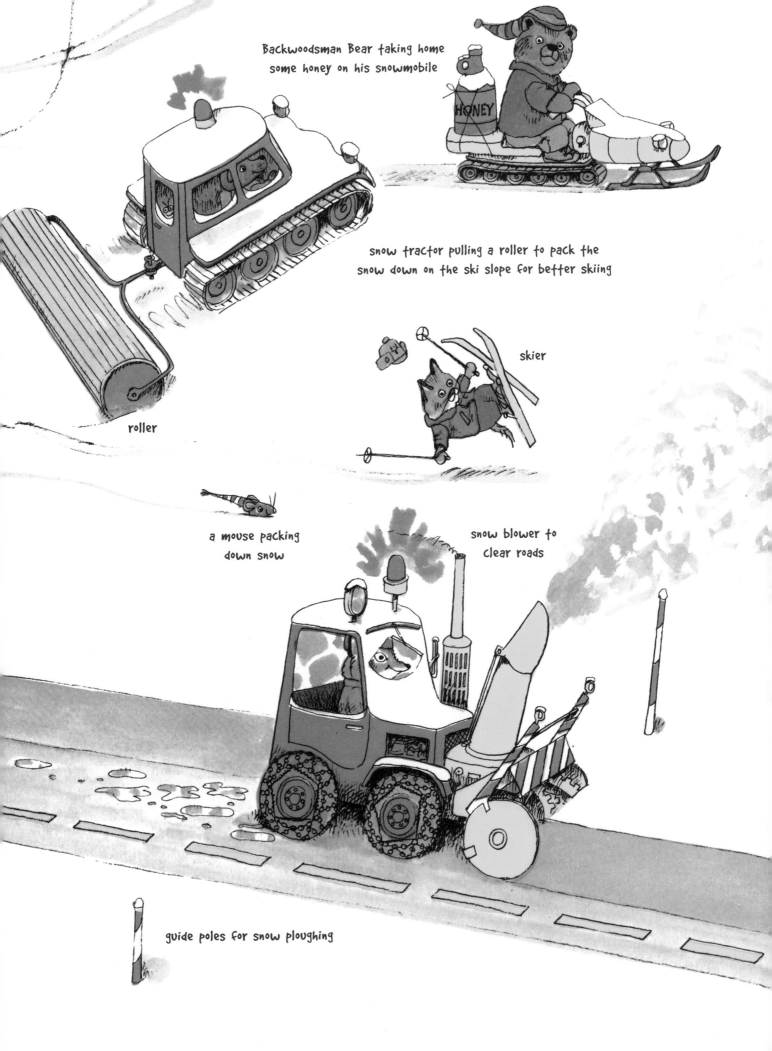

Backwoodsman Bear taking home
some honey on his snowmobile

snow tractor pulling a roller to pack the
snow down on the ski slope for better skiing

skier

roller

a mouse packing
down snow

snow blower to
clear roads

guide poles for snow ploughing

express truck and trailers

EXPRESS 1

tipped-over watermelon truck

STOP!

Did you guess what those things were,
all covered with snow?
Well! Now you KNOW! They are watermelons.
STOP, WATERMELONS, STOP!

Henry, chasing a watermelon

vintage car

cement mixer

The noise of the rolling watermelons
wakens Pa. Ma stops and Pa takes off the sn[ow]
chains. They have come down out of the
mountains, and there is no more snow.
Now Ma is helping Pa put the top down as th[e]
snow is all melted… well, almost all melted[.]

snow chains

runaway watermelons

EXPRESS 2

EXPRESS 3

chemical tanker

mountain climber

Harry, chasing a watermelon

STOP!

carl cat's car

sportscar

skis on a rack

snowshoe

SKI SCHOOL

ski-school bus

Oh, NO!
I never thought I would see an
accident as bad as this one! This is
what I would call SOME ACCIDENT!
It just doesn't seem possible, does it?
But there you are...you can see for yourself.
And poor Mistress Mouse!
It will probably take her a
MILLION YEARS to mend everything.
Luckily, no one was badly hurt.

WHIPPED CREAM

FIRE DE

FLOUR

TOMATO JUICE

BANANAS

FRESH EGGS

MISTRESS MOUSE REPAIRS

The egg men always wear seat belts so that they
won't fall out and get broken. Do you?

"Well, we are almost home now," says Pa. "Thanks goodness," says Ma.

And, sure enough, here they are.
"BACK, SAFE, HOME AGAIN," they all say together.
In front of their house, a delivery man is just leaving.
"What are those boxes on the front lawn?" asks Ma.
"What are those boxes on the front lawn?" asks Penny.
"What are those boxes on the front lawn?" asks Pickles.
Pa just smiles and doesn't ask anything.
"Oh, look!" says Ma. "I think we are going to have new neighbours."
"Oh, goody," say Penny and Pickles.

TOYS

delivery van

advertising ca

COMING SOON
RODEO

THIS SIDE UP

mobile library

YOUR MOBILE LIBRARY
BRINGING BOOKS TO YOU

WELCOME WAGON

And sure enough, Ma is right, as usual. They *do* have new neighbours.
And Penny and Pickles – and Goldbug, too! – have new toy cars.
Pa bought them at the toy shop at the start of their trip.
Do you remember his visit to the toy shop?

Well, at last! Officer Flossy has finally caught that Dingo.
When will he ever learn to drive properly?
Probably never... but we can always hope for the best.
My! Hasn't it been an exciting day?

THIS IS THE END

First published in 1974
This edition published by HarperCollins Children's Books in 2010

HarperCollins Children's Books is a division of HarperCollins Publishers Ltd,
77-85 Fulham Palace Road, London W6 8JB

1 3 5 7 9 10 8 6 4 2

ISBN: 978-0-00-789286-0

The HarperCollins website address is www.harpercollins.co.uk

Printed and bound in China by South China Printing Co.Ltd.